CASEY WEBBER THE GREAT

Story by Hazel Hutchins
Art by John Richmond

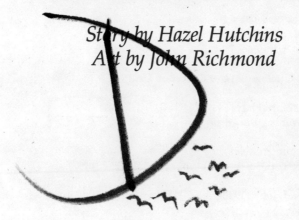

Annick Press Ltd.
Toronto, M2M 1H9

Annick Press gratefully acknowledges
the support of The Canada Council and
the Ontario Arts Council

Canadian Cataloguing in Publication Data

Hutchins, H. J. (Hazel J.)
  Casey Webber, the great

(Annick young novels)
ISBN 1-55037-023-5 (bound) ISBN 1-55037-022-7 (pbk.)

I. Richmond, John, 1926–   . II. Title.
III. Series.

PS8565.U72C38 1988   jC813′.54   C88-094084-0
PZ7.H87Ca 1988

Annick Press trade titles are
distributed in Canada and the USA by:

Firefly Books Ltd.,
3520 Pharmacy Ave., Unit 1C
Scarborough, Ontario
M1W 2T8

Printed and bound in Canada

To Wil,
Who has a magic
all his own

Chapter One

*A*round and around and around and around.

Like a giant's pinwheel left forgotten on the grass, the whirl-a-round at the playground on Larch Street was spinning. Its bright colours melted and blurred. Its handrails flew faster and faster.

Around and around and around and around.

In the house backing onto the playground Mrs. Clarissa Armstrong — tall, graceful, and white-haired, looked out the window and watched the whirl-a-round spin. She saw no child in the park to push it. She heard no wind in the trees that might have, somehow, set it at its giddy pace. And still it spun in the sunlight. Faster it spun. Mrs. Armstrong's telephone began to ring, but she did not turn to answer it. She smiled a small, thoughtful smile, and chose not to answer it at all.

Meanwhile, down the sidewalk along Larch Street itself a lone rock came bouncing.

Flip — roll, roll, roll, plop.

Flip — roll, roll, roll, plop.

It travelled past the Novak's door and past the two houses beside it. At the fourth house it turned up the walk beside the front driveway and came to rest at the bottom of the Webber family's front steps. Mrs. Webber found it a thoughtful looking rock as she came out. She bent and picked it up and held it in the palm of her hand a moment before setting it on the edge of the urn next to the flower bed.

"Casey! Casey!" she called.

Casey Weber appeared in the doorway of the garage. He was 10½ years old that summer, with brown hair and brown eyes and size seven sneakers. He had bright, quick eyes and an easy grin and if he had any faults at all they were the kind of faults that come of loving life. Casey liked to be in the middle of it, right in the very thick of what was happening. Sometimes life on Larch Street was so slow it seemed like it could never hold him, for Casey had always wanted to be part of bigger things, greater things.

And just that morning, while cleaning out the depths of his bedroom closet, he had found something that could make it all possible.

"There you are," said Casey's mom. "Your sister has left already and I'm just on my way across town now. Are you sure you don't want to come with me?"

"No thanks," said Casey. "I'll be okay."

"You know where to reach me?" asked Mrs. Webber.

Casey nodded.

"All right. Take care," said Mrs. Webber.

She climbed into the car, backed it out of the driveway and, with a wave, drove off down the street.

Casey went back into the garage. The thoughtful brown rock stayed on the edge of the urn. The whirl-a-round at the park made its last, heavily-graceful turn and finally stopped.

It was about ten minutes later that Casey began to drag things out of the garage and set them up on the front lawn. The old lemonade stand was first. The old ropes and blankets were next. Casey tied and draped them between trees to make a shelter. For the floor he

laid down a
couple of sacks
stuffed inside each other.
Last of all he brought out a piece
of cardboard and a lawn chair. He drew a
sign on the cardboard and leaned it against
the shelter beneath the trees. He sat down in
the lawn chair to wait.

After only a short while the door of one
of the houses across the street opened and Mrs.
Armstrong appeared. She came strolling out of
her house and down the walk with her special
lemonade hat, her oversize purse and her own
lawn chair. In the old days, when Casey and his
sister Morgan still had had lemonade stands
together, Mrs. Armstrong had always been
their number one customer. Casey had been
counting on Mrs. Armstrong.

"Hello Casey," she said, setting up the
lawn chair beside his own. "I thought you were
too old for lemonade stands these days. I'm
glad to see you're not."

Casey liked Mrs. Armstrong. He
was sorry now that he hadn't thought of
serving refreshments.

"Actually I'm not selling lemonade," said Casey.

"No?" asked Mrs. Armstrong.

"It's a magic show," said Casey, pointing to the sign. "It costs 25 cents but you're my first customer, so you can watch for free."

"Thank you Casey," said Mrs. Armstrong. "Where do I sit?"

"Here is fine," said Casey. "I'm going to go into my magic chamber. As soon as I do, you count to twenty and then you come and be amazed."

"Amazed?" asked Mrs. Armstrong.

"Amazed," said Casey.

"Why not," said Mrs. Armstrong. She sat down, straightened her hat, folded her hands and looked up at Casey. "I'm ready when you are."

Casey went into his magic chamber.

"Start counting," he called.

"One, two, three..." began Mrs. Armstrong. She counted all the way up the line. "...eighteen, nineteen, twenty. Ready?"

Casey didn't answer.

Mrs. Armstrong waited a few extra moments, just to be sure. She stood up and crossed the grass to the magic chamber. She just peeked in at first, the way someone does when they're afraid of ruining someone else's fun. Then she took a step forward and peered fully around the doorway. Finally she walked right inside. There was plenty of room for her. Casey wasn't there.

"Casey?" she called.

There was no answer.

"Casey?"

Mrs. Armstrong came out of the magic chamber with a look of pure delight on her face. Carefully eyeing the blankets, she walked all around the outside. She looked up in the trees. There was nowhere, literally nowhere, that a boy with size seven feet could be hiding. Casey appeared to have been absorbed into the very fabric of the magic shelter itself.

Mrs. Armstrong sat down in her lawn chair again.

"Okay, Casey," she called. "you've amazed me."

There was a slight noise in the magic chamber. A moment later Casey walked out. Mrs. Armstrong smiled and smiled when she saw him.

"I don't think anyone would have the faintest idea how you did it!" said Mrs. Armstrong.

"It's a secret," said Casey. "Do you want to see it again?"

"No," said Mrs. Armstrong. "When

something is done perfectly the first time, it doesn't need doing again."

She stood up and folded her lawn chair.

"I think you've got more customers headed your way," she called back over her shoulder as she crossed the sidewalk.

Casey looked up and down the street. There was no one in sight, but Mrs. Armstrong was probably right. She had funny ways of knowing things. Sure enough, less than a minute after she had said goodbye, Casey's good friends Max and T.J. came roaring around the corner on their bicycles. They raced down the street at 100 kph, slammed on the brakes and skidded their bikes to a stop in the Webber's gravel drive.

"Hey Casey!" said Max. "What's up!"

Chapter Two

"When I came home there were 287 people all over the lawn and a crummy stack of boxes and blankets and things. It looked like we'd opened a home for street people or something. Mother, talk to him!"

Casey's sister Morgan put her hands on her hips and glared across the kitchen at her brother. Mrs. Webber had just come in the door. She raised a hand of peace.

"Morgan, whatever it is, if you'll just give him a chance, I'm sure Casey has an explanation," she said.

"There weren't 287 people," said Casey. "There were, maybe, twelve. And I put everything away afterwards."

"He was trying to attract attention the way he always is," said Morgan. "He's been trying to attract attention since the day some crazed person told him he was the cutest elf in the Christmas Concert, when he was six. Tell him he can't attract attention on our front lawn!"

"What were you doing, Casey?"

"It was a magic show," said Casey.

"But you don't know any magic..." began his mom. "Oh, I know — that magic kit we gave you for Christmas. I wondered why you weren't interested in it before. Maybe you can show us some of the tricks."

"Mother!" said Morgan. "I had friends with me. They're all going to be saying I live in a slum!"

"Morgan, it couldn't have been that serious," said their mom.

"Serious? No, it wasn't serious. *Mortifying. Devastating. Degrading.* But not serious," said Morgan. Morgan was the world's most sarcastic sister. She hadn't always been — in fact she and Casey had been good friends at one time. But things had changed.

"It seems to me you're forgetting something, Morgan," said their mother. "You're not supposed to have friends over when I'm not around. If you'd told me, I could have easily arranged to be home. I'd like to meet your friends."

"But what about Casey?" said Morgan.

"He had half the city over while you were gone!"

"Casey," said their mom. "I'm glad you're interested in magic, but next time you want to do something public, please make sure either your dad or I are home. And use the back yard instead of the front."

"Okay," said Casey.

There really wasn't much else he could say. Things had kind of gotten out of control after Max and T.J. had arrived. Max and T.J. had been more than amazed by Casey's magic act. Max and T.J. had been IMPRESSED. They had tied two big signs to their bikes and gone all over advertising that the "World's Greatest Magician" was just around the corner performing one of the "World's Most Amazing Tricks." And people had come.

And seeing it all spelled out in words like that and in the midst of all the people coming and going, Casey had suddenly felt strangely unsure of himself. Of course he'd always wanted to be amazing. Of course he'd always wanted to be the greatest... something. But somehow he had always imagined earning his own way to being Casey the Great — it wasn't supposed to happen now. Tomorrow, maybe. Things looked a lot different when you thought of them as happening "now".

"What's this?" asked their mother. She turned with a piece of paper in her hand.

"It's a telegram," said Morgan. "They phoned it to us just before you came in."

"COMING SOONEST. STRONGLY SUGGEST YOU LET WELL ENOUGH ALONE. S.V." read Mrs. Webber aloud. "That's odd. Are you sure you got it right, Morgan?"

"Mother, I got it right," said Morgan.

"But who is it from? We don't know anyone with the initials S.V.," said Mrs. Webber.

"Maybe it's a joke," said Morgan.

"It's worded more like a threat than a joke," said Mrs. Webber.

"That's it!" said Morgan. "It makes perfect sense. Mr. Magic out on the front lawn. Threatening telegrams over the phone. Any minute now the doorbell will ring and the Mounties will walk in and take us all away."

Morgan shuffled off into the living room.

"Casey, sometimes I wish your sister wouldn't be quite so . . ."

But Casey wasn't there.

Casey had gone down to his bedroom. He carefully closed his door and then went into

16

his closet and pulled out the old dress-up box. It didn't look much like a dress-up box any more. It was filled to overflowing with small plastic packages of ketchup — souvenirs of almost every hot dog Casey ever ate. Casey reached beneath the ketchup packages and pulled out a jacket.

It was brown in colour with just enough fine gold threads running through it to suggest that in better days it would have had a soft golden sheen. The collar was high and rounded. The buttons were metal and of intricate design. On the breast was a small, shield-shaped area of brighter fabric where a crest must once have been attached. When they were very young, he and Morgan had played all sorts of wonderful, impossible games with this very jacket. But it hadn't been until this morning, when he'd found the jacket lost and forgotten at the back of his closet, that Casey had realized those wonderful games had been real.

"The lady at the Christmas concert only said you were the cutest elf because you tripped over the sleigh and she felt sorry for you!"

Casey spun around. Morgan had opened the bedroom door and stuck her head in. "Morgan!" said Casey. He tried to cram the

jacket back
under the
plastic ketchup packages.

"Sorry, I forgot to knock. We normal people sometimes forget to knock," said Morgan. "What's that?"

"Nothing," said Casey.

"Yes it is," said Morgan. "It's the old magic jacket. I didn't know we still had it."

"We don't," said Casey.

A little light of understanding came into Morgan's eyes.

"Oh for Pete's sake, Casey. You don't still believe in it, do you?"

"Of course not," said Casey. His heart was thumping somewhere up around his ears. "Of course not!"

"Yes you do," said Morgan. "Oh Casey, sometimes I don't think you're ever going to grow up."

Before Casey could even think what to do she stepped into the room, reached out and took the jacket.

There, in the doorway of Casey's bedroom, Morgan put on the jacket. And there, in the doorway of Casey's bedroom, she disappeared. She didn't fade or tingle or spark. She just slid

cleanly, perfectly, completely out of view.

"See," said Morgan. "It really works. I'm invisible."

Casey saw. She was invisible all right. It truly was amazing. But the most amazing thing of all was that Morgan was still being sarcastic. She didn't seem to know she was invisible.

Then Casey remembered. Of course, she couldn't know — she could still see herself. That was the way the jacket worked! She could still see her hands and feet and clothes. Only the mirror out of sight around the corner of the room or Casey himself could tell her anything different — and Casey wasn't talking. Whatever plans he might have for the jacket, he was certain they wouldn't include his sister.

A moment later Morgan slid into view again as she took off the jacket. "Casey, you really amaze me," she said. She handed him the jacket, rolled her eyes in melodramatic disgust and left the room.

With a sigh of relief, Casey sank back on the bed with the jacket in his arms. He knew for sure now. He did want to use the jacket. He had just seen with his own eyes its clear and perfect magic. Something about it spoke to him this morning, when he had first found the jacket. It spoke to him like a song, or a challenge.

"See what I can do?" it seemed to say. "Catch me if you can, Casey Webber. Match me if you can."

Casey bent over, and took from the floor something small and flat and metal. From where it was lying it might have fallen from the jacket itself, except Casey had checked the pockets that morning and they had all been empty. As he turned it in his hands he saw that it was a case, really, and beneath the hinged lid was a picture of a man with a broad face, a wide flat nose, and a small, well-trimmed beard.

Casey set the object on his dresser. Later, if Morgan did not come back to claim it, perhaps he would look at it again. Right now he was going to find the old magic kit his mom and dad had given him. After all, if he was going to be the world's greatest magician, he had to have more than one trick.

Chapter Three

*T*he rope lay neatly coiled on the warm green grass of Shaughnessy Park. Around the rope was a hula-hoop. Around the hula-hoop were 30 children, all younger than Casey, sitting in a semi-circle on the grass.

"Today we have a special guest," said the young girl with the T-shirt that read SU-SAN across the front and SHAUGHNESSY PARK across the back. "He's going to treat us to a magic show."

Susan was leader of the Summer Fun Program. Casey had gone to the Summer Fun Program at Shaughnessy himself when he was younger and Susan and Casey had always got along well together. When he'd explained about how he had been banished from the front yard yesterday, Susan had agreed to let him try out his act at the park.

"But I warn you," Susan had cautioned, "they're great kids, but a tough audience."

Now, as he stood before them, Casey saw what Susan meant. Only two of the children looked even mildly interested. Ten of them looked completely bored. Fourteen were looking at grass, trees, freckles, warts — anything other than Casey. And one boy in a yellow shirt had already announced that he hated magic shows and was sure Casey was going to mess up anyway.

Casey took a deep breath and jumped in with both feet.

"This rope is going to dance," he said. "All you have to do is count to forty and say the magic words, Alakazee, Alakazam."

"Alaka — yuck," said old yellow shirt.

"One..." began a little girl.

"Wait," said Casey, holding up a hand. "I must warn you that if you go inside the hoop the magic will be broken. Remember — Alakazee, Alakazam. Count."

"One .... two ....
...... three..."

"Keep counting!" called Casey as he stepped back into the picnic shelter. "Alakazee. Alakazam!"

The children kept counting. They were slow counters but finally they made it to the thirties.

"Thirty-eight . . . . thirty-nine . . . . FORTY."

Twenty-nine voices shouted, "ALA-KAZEE! ALAKAZAM!"

One voice shouted, "ALAKA — YUCK."

The rope in the centre of the hula-hoop lay still and lifeless.

"He's messed up. I knew he would," said old yellow shirt.

Just as he spoke, however, the very tip of the rope moved. It wasn't much, just a little jerk of a movement, and then the rope again lay still.

Yellow shirt leaned over and waved his hands back and forth over the rope to check for strings. He reached out and poked the rope with a finger.

"Leave it alone. You'll wreck it!" said another child.

Yellow shirt pulled his hand back. The children waited.

Again the end of the rope lifted — a little stronger this time, a little higher. It wavered slightly and slid back to earth, but almost

immediately it rose
again. Weaving back and forth
with a rhythmical motion this time,
slowly, slowly, it began to climb.

"I hear something!" said one
of the children.

There was indeed a sound.
From the trees, the grass, the very
air around the rope there came the
sound of primitive music not un-
like the buzz of a kazoo. Flat and
tuneless at first, it gradually became strong and more melodic
— the song of the Indian snake
charmer.

All but the very tail of
the snake rope had lifted
itself from the ground
now. Back and forth,
back and forth it
swayed in time to the
music.

Suddenly the tune changed.

It began to boogie and the snake rope began to boogie too.

The kids giggled. The rope struck out playfully. The kids laughed. The rope jiggled and jived. It coiled itself into knots, it made itself into loops, it bopped and boogied, jumped into the air, did a triple flip, a double circle, a grand whirl and a high-flying quadruple whirly-bird for a grand finale.

Ta Daaaaa!

The children clapped. The rope stood straight at attention, broke at the middle and bowed. It curled on the grass and became lifeless once again.

When Casey stepped out of the picnic shelter, several of the kids were holding the rope.

"Did it work?" asked Casey.

Everyone answered all at once and told him what the rope had done. Finally one little girl, with dark hair and dark eyes came up to him and held out the rope.

"Could you make it happen again

please?" she asked. "I've never seen real magic before."

Casey looked at her. She had asked so simply and earnestly that he almost said yes. He remembered Mrs. Armstrong's words, however. When something is done well the first time, it shouldn't be done again. Even regular magicians followed that rule.

"Maybe I could come again and do something else," said Casey as he shook his head.

"Yes please," said May.

She placed the rope in Casey's hands. The magic had been returned to the magician. The show was properly over.

"Fox-and-goose time, everyone. Last one down on the field is the fox!" called Susan's helper.

As the children raced away after him, Susan stayed behind a moment to speak with Casey.

"Well done, Casey!" she said. "The kids really enjoyed it — May Tanagami especially. She's such a shy kid, she doesn't usually speak to anyone. Come back anytime, okay?"

"Could I come tomorrow?" asked Casey.

"Same time?" said Susan.

27

Casey coiled the rope around his neck and headed off on his bike. There was a bright bubble of elation just beneath his ribs that made him fairly fly down the road. He hadn't meant the rope to jive and bop and boogie — he'd just meant to make it rise up from the ground and go back down to the sound of the kazoo. Things had gotten a bit carried away again.

But the children at the park had liked it. What had the girl named May said? "Real magic." That was exactly what the jacket was — real magic, with Casey Webber's own special touch!

Chapter Four

*C*asey was still at swimming lessons a few mornings later, when Max and T.J. stopped over to see when his next magic show was going to be.

"You should see him," Max told Morgan. "He's great!"

"But what exactly does he do?" asked Morgan.

"Last night he cast a spell on T.J.'s hat and made it float all over the back yard. And he wasn't even near the hat. He was out front somewhere!" said Max.

"I think he did it with remote-control magnets," said T.J.

"And a couple of days before that, on the lawn, that was the greatest," said Max. "He disappeared. He just went into this little hut he'd made and when we looked inside — he wasn't there."

"He was probably hiding behind a blanket or something," said Morgan.

"Nope," said Max. "We checked — everywhere. Then a few minutes later — there he was again."

"Where?"

"In the hut. He just came walking out," said Max.

"I think there must be a tunnel under your front lawn somewhere that we couldn't find," said T.J.

"Right. We have tunnels all over this place. It's mole city," said Morgan.

"Nope, that sort of stuff is done with mirrors," said Max. "I don't know how, but it's neat. Casey's going to get a whole magic show together and be the world's greatest magician."

"He is?" asked Morgan.

"It'll be awesome," said T.J. "I'll be living on the same street as him. People will ask, 'Did you see Casey Abernathie Webber on T.V. last night?' and I'll say, 'See him on T.V.! Heck, I see him every day. He's a buddy of mine.'"

"And you'll be his sister!" said Max.

"I'm his sister already," said Morgan.

"Yeah, but you'll be the sister of the great magician," said Max. "When does he get back from swimming lessons?"

"Noon," said Morgan. "And he's got them every day this week and next week and you know it, so stop hanging around here in the mornings. Goodbye."

Having ended the conversation, Morgan abruptly closed the door. Max and T.J. were left on the steps outside.

"Morgan never used to be like that," said Max. "Something's up."

When Max and T.J. had gone, Morgan went into the living room, turned on the T.V. set and sat down in front of it. There was a game show on and Morgan hated game shows, but she stared at it determinedly anyway. She was trying not to think. There were a lot of things going on in Morgan's life lately, and she found that the more she thought about them, the more mixed up she became. And on top of it all she had to have a brother who cast spells and disappeared on the front lawn.

Morgan stared even harder at the T.V. Disappearing on the front lawn and floating hats — of course it was crazy! She had tried on the jacket herself to prove it was crazy. And yet... and yet, there were things Morgan could remember. Games she and Casey had played a long, long time ago.

For a few more moments Morgan stared at the T.V. She didn't know it, but she was trying very hard to hypnotize herself into a safe state of disbelief. Finally she gave up. She turned off the T.V. and went upstairs to Casey's bedroom. She looked in the closet under the ketchup collection first, and under the bed and in the secret place behind Casey's desk. Last of all she began opening dresser drawers. Neatly folded, in the third drawer down between the T-shirts and the jeans, she found the jacket.

* * *

When Casey got home from swimming lessons, the first thing he did was go to the bedroom and check on his jacket. It was fine. Casey went to the kitchen. Morgan had already left the house but his dad was home. He and Casey had lunch together on the back deck.

"Dad, if somebody was really good at something — juggling or singing or tap dancing or..."

"...magic," filled in Casey's dad.

"Or magic," said Casey. "How would they get to be famous?"

"Casey, I don't think you need to

worry about that yet," said his dad. "You're just beginning."

"But just supposing they really were the best. The very best."

"Well, I have to think about this. I've never been famous, you know," said Casey's dad. "I suppose some people enter contests. Some people put ads in the paper or go door to door to places that might want to hire them. Some people go to agents who do the bookings for them."

"But that takes a lot of time," said Casey.

"Of course it does," said his dad. "That's half the point. You learn as you go along."

"But what if you were soooo good you didn't need to learn any more? What if you were the most amazing, most stupendous, most astounding and truly magical act ever?"

"Then you'd have to write to Tom Gregory," said his dad.

"Who?" asked Casey.

"Tom Gregory. He's a talk show host on late night T.V. If you get on the Tom Gregory show — you're famous."

"What's his address?" asked Casey.

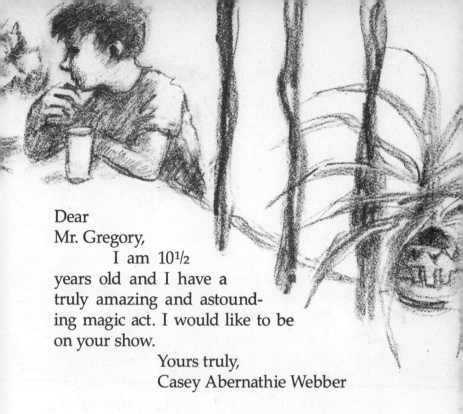

Dear
Mr. Gregory,
      I am 10½
years old and I have a
truly amazing and astounding magic act. I would like to be
on your show.
                    Yours truly,
                    Casey Abernathie Webber

      Casey wrote the letter when he got
back from Shaughnessy Park that afternoon.
He also wrote to the local T.V. amateur hour,
just in case Tom Gregory didn't want him. Last
of all he wrote a letter to an agency that ran an
ad in the city paper saying they supplied magicians, jugglers and entertainers of all sorts for
parties and other festive events. They called
themselves "Entertainers At Large" and Casey
decided that if they supplied people for parties,
they had to hire them in the first place.

Casey's mom was sitting at her desk when Casey went into the living room to get some stamps from the desk drawer. She was supposed to be working on some estimates, but she was looking out the window instead.

Down at the corner of the block Morgan and three friends were talking in a small, closed circle.

"Casey, do you know why Morgan never brings her friends by the house any more?" asked Casey's mom.

"Nope," said Casey.

"Neither do I," said his mom. "I've tried talking to her about it but . . . well, Morgan and I don't seem to be able to talk these days."

Casey took three stamps out of the drawer and stuck them on his three envelopes. Each stamp seemed to be the seal on the promise of greatness to come.

"A police cruiser," said his mom. "That's the second one I've seen drive past here this week. I don't like it. Something's going on."

Casey looked out the window. There was indeed a police cruiser passing like a silent shadow on the street. It slowed as it passed the Webber house, idled down to the end of the block and turned the corner.

"Maybe Morgan's right. Maybe the Mounties are after us."

"It's not funny," said Mrs. Webber. "Another telegram came today. The telegraph office can't trace where it came from. Your dad can't make sense of it any more than I can."

Casey glanced at the yellow and purple paper his mom held out in her hand.

"DELAYED. STRONGLY, REPEAT, STRONGLY ADVISE YOU CEASE ACTION. S.V."

"Doesn't make any sense to me," said Casey, and went off to mail his letters.

Chapter Five

*M*ay Tanagami was floating. On the grass in front of the picnic shelter at Shaughnessy Park her body rested in a position of semi-recline about two feet off the ground. It wasn't a particularly graceful sight — she wasn't all laid out flat and perfect like in the big magic shows — but it was an interesting sight nonetheless. Besides, what was lost in grace was more than made up for by movement. She floated up, down, around, back and forth and finally landed, with a slight bump, on the ground again.

"What did it feel like?" asked one of the new kids as May walked back to her spot on the grass afterwards.

"She won't tell you. May doesn't talk," said old yellow shirt.

May, however, paused just before she

sat down. She looked at the boy with the yellow shirt and then at the boy who had asked the question.

"It felt like I was being held by some . . . by something that wouldn't let me fall. It felt safe," she said.

She sat down on the grass and hugged her knees and stared at Casey with great shining eyes.

"Hey, Casey. Make me float!" called yellow shirt.

"Not today," said Casey.

Every afternoon for the past week Casey had come to the park and tried out ideas for his magic show. It had all been an enormous success. He had made hula-hoops and pack sacks dance, caused musical instruments to play themselves, sneaked surprise bubble gum into unsuspecting pockets, made bicycles race riderless across the park and caused a number of other amazing occurrences. But he never did the same trick twice. Today Casey had an audition with "Entertainers At Large."

"Are you nervous?" asked Susan as Casey was packing up.

"I'm not sure," said Casey. "I think I'm mostly excited."

He slipped on his pack sack. It held the

things he was going to use for his audition and was bigger than usual. Susan helped him pull it over his shoulders.

"Good luck," she said. "Don't forget us when you're rich and famous."

*   *   *

The address was right downtown in one of the few old sandstone buildings still standing. Casey climbed the stairs to the third floor. For just a moment he stood before the door with its clouded glass and block lettering. When he next came out of that door, his life would be forever changed. He would enter as Casey the kid. He would emerge as Casey Webber the Great. He turned the knob and stepped in.

There were two very ordinary desks inside, with two very ordinary looking people working at them. This was slightly disappointing. Casey had expected there to be at least some small excitement. A rock band or a performing dog or even a stand-up comedian or two would have been nice.

He was shown through to a second office and introduced to Amanda A. Bates. Mrs. Bates was sleek and sharp looking and sat behind a desk strewn with paper and photo-

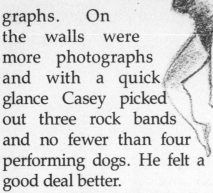

graphs. On
the walls were
more photographs
and with a quick
glance Casey picked
out three rock bands
and no fewer than four
performing dogs. He felt a
good deal better.

"Casey Webber, age 10½, amazing
and astounding magic," read Mrs. Bates as she
glanced at one of the papers on her desk. "Did
Mick explain on the phone that we only book
serious, professional acts? Do you still want to
go through with this?"

''Yes
please," said
Casey.

"Someone has written here that you need a table," said Mrs. Bates. "You can use the one in the corner."

Casey pulled the table forward and draped the front of it with his sheet. On top of the table he set most of the things from his pack sack, including the rope from his old magic kit, a cup, a bottle of water and a large orange and blue parrot puppet.

"Can I start now?" he asked.

"Go right ahead," said Mrs. Bates. "Amaze and astound me."

Casey ducked beneath the table.

"Alakazee, alakazam!"

The primitive, kazoo-like music began and the rope on the table began to dance.

"Alakazee, alakazam!"

The cup and water bottle on the table floated up into the air. The bottle poured water into the cup. The cup poured water into the air where it vanished with a slight gurgling sound.

"Alakazee, alakazam!"

The parrot came to life. He walked across the table, squawked twice, flew around the room and landed beak-first in a potted plant.

A few seconds later Casey emerged from beneath the table. Mrs. Bates was looking at the parrot with an intensely thoughtful expression.

"How do you like it so far?" asked Casey.

Mrs. Bates jumped. Her eyes swung around to meet Casey's.

"Is there more?" she asked.

"Lots more," said Casey. "A harmonica that plays itself, scissors cutting out paper dolls, a chalkboard that writes down anything you tell it to write..."

"Wait," said Mrs. Bates, raising a hand. "Wait. Is it all done the same way? I mean, are you under the table for the whole act?"

"No," said Casey.

"Yes," said Casey.

"Kind of," said Casey. "Does it matter? It's magic!"

"Yes, I know it's magic," said Mrs. Bates. "It's even mildly entertaining in its own way but, you see, the whole point of a magic show is that the audience can see the magician perform the trick. That's the whole point."

"But...mine doesn't work that way," stammered Casey.

Mrs. Bates seemed to consider this for a moment.

"Perhaps if you didn't try to fool people," she suggested. "Perhaps if you announced it as a puppet show and made up a story and..."

"A puppet show!" said Casey. He could hardly believe what he was hearing. "It's not a puppet show! It's not even like a puppet show or anything to do with a puppet show. It's..."

Mrs. Bates lifted her shoulders in a way that managed to be both regretful and final.

"You mean you don't even want to see any more?" asked Casey.

"It wouldn't be any use," said Mrs. Bates. "I've been in this business thirty years. I know what I can market and what I can't. The way your act is now, it doesn't work."

Casey opened his mouth and closed it several times. He couldn't think of anything to say.

Mechanically, he picked up his gear and packed it back into his pack sack. He said goodbye and walked out the door and through the outer office and out the second door and half way down the stairs without really looking where he was going at all, and that's why he tripped over the person standing there. He fell down the last few steps and crashed on the landing.

"My goodness! Casey!" said a voice. "Are you hurt?"

"No, I'm all right," said Casey. He rubbed his knee and slowly picked himself up. "Oh, hi Mrs. Armstrong. What are you doing here? Are you going for an interview too?"

"Me? No. I'm going to get my teeth fixed. Old building, old dentist, — I'm the old patient. What sort of interview?"

"Just an interview," said Casey.

"It sounds as if it didn't go so well," said Mrs. Armstrong.

"It didn't," said Casey.

"Well, there's always more than one way to do things, whatever it is — but you have to believe in yourself. You remember that, Casey. You're sure you're all right?"

"I'm all right," said Casey

Mrs. Armstrong stood looking at him.

"Aren't you going to your appointment?" he asked.

"I suppose I'd better," said Mrs. Armstrong. "Take care now."

"Bye," said Casey.

He walked out into the flow of people

along the sidewalk, just letting them carry him along. When he was far enough from the old sandstone building to be able to think clearly again, he climbed up on the back of a bench and sat watching the people go by.

Really, he thought, it didn't make sense to be disappointed about Mrs. Bates. He still had the jacket — an incredible, impossible, magical jacket with which he could make himself invisible any time and any place. There were all sorts of possibilities besides going around and amazing people. He could become a spy. He could rob banks. He could go anywhere, do anything. In a way, he could almost be anybody.

Casey sighed and shook his head. Maybe Morgan was right. Maybe it all came from the lady who said he was the cutest elf in the Christmas Concert. All he knew was that out of all the possibilities — the spies, robbers, practical jokers and anything else — the way he'd chosen was the right way for Casey Webber. It had his style stamped all over it.

And he wasn't about to give up.

Chapter Six

*F*OR HIRE OR RENT:
FIRST CLASS MAGICIAN
Casey looked at what he'd written, drew a line through it, and tried again.
MAGICIAN FOR HIRE: BIRTHDAY PARTIES, STAGE SHOWS, OCCASIONS OF STATE.
He read, crossed out, began again.
WORLD'S MOST AMAZING MAGICIAN WITH WORLD'S MOST AMAZING AND TRULY MAGICAL ACT FOR HIRE. CHEAP.
Casey sighed and chewed on the end of his pencil. No one could possibly say what he wanted to say in 10 words or less, and 10 words of a newspaper ad were all he could afford. If only the local amateur hour or, better yet, the Tom Gregory Show would answer his letters. Somehow, this time, he would make them understand.

The door to his room opened. Morgan stuck her head around the corner. She looked at Casey and frowned.

"Why aren't you swimming?" she asked.

"My lessons are finished," said Casey.

Morgan hesitated. "Well," she said, "I don't suppose it really matters."

She crossed to the dresser, opened the third drawer down and took the jacket. She was halfway out the door before Casey really understood.

"Morgan!"

Morgan paused and looked back at Casey.

"I need it," she said.

"You can't have it," said Casey. "It's my jacket."

"It's our jacket," said Morgan. "And don't get all worried because I know how it works and everything and I'll give it back."

She turned and walked out of the room. Casey sprang after her.

"What do you mean you know about it?" asked Casey following hard on her heels down the hall.

"I know," said Morgan.

"But . . ."

Morgan had turned into her room. She tried to sandwich Casey in the doorway, but it was really only a half-hearted attempt and Casey pushed through.

"You mean you *know*?" asked Casey.

"Is there an echo in here?" asked Morgan.

She opened the closet door and drew aside her clothes on their hangers. On the floor behind them, stacked neatly on the shelves and on top of each other and everywhere else, were...things. New things. Unused things. They were things, Casey knew, which Morgan could not afford to buy with her allowance or any other way. There were clothes, shoes, records, cameras, and tennis racquets. He could see six hair dryers, all sorts of jewellery and an enormous brass candelabra. Casey stared. Morgan herself stared. She threw up her arms.

"How am I going to carry all this stuff all the way to the mall!" she said.

Casey didn't answer. There weren't six blow dryers. There were eight. Morgan looked at him.

"Do you still have your big wagon?" she asked.

Casey looked at Morgan.

"You're perfectly right. I stole it all,"

said Morgan. "All of it. You're the world's greatest magician. I'm the world's greatest shoplifter. I did it every morning while you were swimming. Fun, isn't it? All my friends think shoplifting is the neatest trick to do."

"Morgan..." began Casey.

"Only I can't stand it any more," said Morgan. "It's dumb and it's wrong and I don't care if they think it's cool. I think they're stupid and I'm taking all this stuff back. Right now before I lose my nerve. Do you still have your wagon?"

"Do your friends know about the jacket?" asked Casey.

"No. They think talented Morgan Webber lifted all this wonderful junk by herself. Your secret's safe," said Morgan. "What about the wagon?"

Casey went along with Morgan to the shopping mall. Morgan didn't tell him to get lost, so he figured he was invited. For two hours he watched Morgan return merchandise to the stores from which she'd taken it. It was quite fascinating. At times, as he stood by the wagon, things would float discreetly out of the bags and zip away. They would fly low to the ground down the aisles and close to displays until they came to rest wherever they had been stolen from. At other times he and a perfectly visible Morgan would load up with merchandise and then Casey would help her put on the jacket. So long as she was holding the items at the time she put on the jacket, everything — including Morgan herself — disappeared. It was in this way that Casey, with great interest, was able to watch the magical reappearance of a large brass candelabra in the window of one of the furniture stores.

Finally they stopped in front of Savoy's Gift Shop. A small sign in the window read "We Prosecute Shoplifters." At the bottom of a bag inside the wagon, its Savoy price tag still attached, was a single silk scarf.

"Well, this is it," said Morgan picking up the scarf. "My doom."

Casey held out the jacket, but Morgan shook her head.

"I stole this scarf live and in person," she said grimly. "When I got caught I put on the jacket and escaped, but Mr. Savoy knows what I look like and he knows what I did, even if he doesn't know my name. I'm going to take it back in person and clear myself for good and always, I hope."

The store was empty of customers. Behind the counter was a young woman. For a moment Morgan's spirits lifted. Maybe, just maybe, she would be lucky after all. As she was explaining the situation to the clerk, however, Mr. Savoy himself came out of the back room. Recognizing Morgan immediately, he crossed to the till and listened for a moment. His expression did not change.

"Come with me," he said.

The clerk gave Morgan a look of sympathy. Morgan turned and followed Mr. Savoy.

In a small office in the back storeroom she was offered a chair while Mr. Savoy settled himself behind the desk. His manner was brisk and firm.

"We prosecute shoplifters in this store," said Mr. Savoy. "We don't accept excuses or apologies of any sort. I know you won't think so now, but it really is for your own good. I want you to fill out this form, neatly, yourself. I'll phone across to security."

He handed Morgan the form and a pen, then he reached for the phone.

That is, he tried to reach for the phone. The phone, for its part, slid away from him.

Mr. Savoy frowned. He reached again. The phone slid away again.

Calmly, the older man returned his

hands to the desk before him. He tidied a pile of invoices. He placed a pen just so. He adjusted his glasses. He opened and shut a small drawer. Like a flash, he grabbed at the phone and pinned it down.

He tried to pick up the receiver. It wouldn't budge. Something was holding it down. Something was holding his whole hand down!

"This is ridiculous!" said Mr. Savoy.

With a jerk, he sprung himself free. The phone toppled off the desk. It slid across the carpet and jammed itself firmly behind a filing cabinet. Mr. Savoy did not try to pick it up.

"Wait here," he said to Morgan. "I'll use the phone out front."

That's when the little office went wild.

The door slammed shut. The lights flashed on, off, on. A stapler began to chatter. Three books flew off the desk. Paper began to swirl and dance in the air.

"What on earth...ack!" A paperweight zoomed past Mr. Savoy's ear.

"Look out!" cried Morgan.

Mr. Savoy ducked and a ledger went sailing just over his head. With a helpless gasp he fell back in his chair, staring wide-eyed at the swirling papers, the swinging light fixtures, the banging drawers, the pencils that zoomed and careened and the dancing pictures. His face became whiter and whiter.

"Casey, stop!" cried Morgan. "Please, stop!"

With a flourish a pen did a final figure 8 above the desk and landed perfectly in a coffee cup. The room fell silent.

"I'm sorry, Mr. Savoy," said Morgan, reaching out to try and straighten things on the desk before the stricken shop owner. "It's my brother. He doesn't really mean anything by it — he's just trying to help. It's all right. It won't happen again."

One or two of the papers lying around picked themselves up and sailed gently, if slightly rumpled, back on the desk.

Mr. Savoy, still very white and wide-eyed, took several large deep breaths of air and ran a hand through his hair.

"Perhaps..." he said. "Perhaps... just this once... it would be better..."

He reached a shaky hand across the desk. Morgan handed him the form she'd been filling out. Mr. Savoy ripped the form in several pieces and placed them, very gingerly, in the wastepaper basket which had floated conveniently over to receive them.

"You mean...I can go?" asked Morgan.

"Yes," said Mr. Savoy, clearing his throat. "Yes. You may go."

Morgan breathed the largest sigh of relief.

"Thank you, Mr. Savoy," she said. "You won't be sorry."

Quickly Morgan stood and opened the door. She held it ajar a moment as if to let someone pass through ahead of her, then, thanking Mr. Savoy one last time she, too, slipped out.

Casey and Morgan walked home side by side, with the empty wagon rattling behind. There were lots of things they could have talked about, but neither said a word.

When they reached home, their mom was sitting on the front steps. She watched them pull the wagon up the walk and into the garage. Then they went inside. When Mrs. Webber came in she found them sitting at the table eating peanut butter and pickle sandwiches. She sat down across from Morgan.

"Did you return everything?" she asked.

Morgan's mouth dropped open.

"You mean you knew about it?" she asked.

"Only since yesterday. I didn't want to start accusing you until I'd talked to your dad, but things were definitely at the point of drastic action," said Mrs. Webber. "You did the right thing, both of you."

"Casey didn't steal anything," said Morgan. "He was just helping me take the stuff back. I was almost brave enough to go it alone but not quite."

"It isn't always easy to do the right thing," said Mrs. Webber.

It was just the kind of sappy thing mothers say, but for once Morgan didn't argue.

"Well," she said, glancing across at Casey. "It could have ended a whole lot worse."

And Casey grinned.

Chapter Seven

*D*ear Casey Webber,

Thank you for your letter. The earliest audition time for KIDS IN THE SPOTLIGHT, our local talent show, is two years next March at 2:30 p.m. on Friday the 17th. We look forward to seeing you then.

Casey stared at the letter in disbelief. Two years next March!

He went to Morgan's room, knocked on the door and walked in. Morgan had been feeling a lot better about life in general since returning all the stuff, but she hadn't quite been brave enough to face her friends yet.

She was working on her third jigsaw puzzle in two days, a picture of a heavy horse pull at a country fair.

Casey handed her the letter.

"Two years!" she said.

"It's really beginning to get to me,"

said Casey, flopping down on the bed. "I could astound all sorts of people if someone would just give me a chance."

Morgan looked out across the jumble of puzzle pieces.

"Casey, besides wanting to amaze people, don't you ever wonder where the jacket came from?" she asked.

"I know where it came from," said Casey. "It came from the old dress-up box."

"I mean before that. It must have come from somewhere. There aren't such things as invisible jackets in the world," said Morgan.

"Yes there are," said Casey. "There's one in my dresser drawer right now."

Morgan picked up a horse's left ear and snapped it into place. She cradled her chin in her hand and looked across at Casey.

"It's old," said Morgan. "You can tell that just from looking at it."

"Probably," said Casey.

"Old as in very old," said Morgan.

"Maybe," said Casey.

"And it's worn," said Morgan, "worn as in it's been worn before."

Casey didn't answer.

"Casey," pressed Morgan. "It might just matter, you know."

"It probably does matter," he said. "It's

just that...Morgan if I start thinking about it I'm afraid I won't use the jacket. I'll think I'm doing it all wrong or I'll think it's meant for someone else or maybe I'll just stop believing in it entirely the way we did before. And that's not right because the jacket is more than just a neat trick — it's magic. It's special. It's the gift of a lifetime and it was in my dress-up box."

"Our dress-up box," said Morgan.

"Our dress-up box," said Casey. "If you want to use it any time...."

Morgan shook her head.

"I have enough trouble just getting along in real life without worrying about being invisible," she replied.

Casey stood up, picked up his letter and walked to the door.

"You aren't going to go spilling the beans to anyone about the jacket, are you, Morgan?" he asked.

"No," she said. "It's funny. Even though I know it's real, there are times when I still find myself just not believing. However it got here, it's ours to use or not to use, but it isn't ours to go blabbing about. But I am going to try and find out where it came from. One of us should at least know that much."

Casey went to his own room. He took the jacket out. Knowing it as well as he did now, just the weight of it in his hands filled him with a special feeling. He straightened the collar and ran his fingers over the fine golden threads. Morgan was right about it. It was old and it was worn. There was history in it.

There was, however, something that Casey had not mentioned. The jacket wasn't quite the same as when he'd first pulled it out of the old dress up box. Its shape was changing. One day an arm would be too long and then it would draw back to Casey's size again. Another day the back would hang down almost to his knees only to later fit properly again. It was not a problem, the jacket still worked perfectly, but it seemed to be moving towards a different shape. It seemed to be telling Casey that not only did it have a past life, it had a future life as well. Only the little time in between belonged to Casey Abernathie Webber.

Casey turned to the window. Mrs. Armstrong was passing on the street. Her lemonade hat was cocked at a jaunty angle and her oversize purse was slung over her arm.

He held the jacket up so that the sunlight fell across the fine sheen of threads.

He wondered if the time in between was going to be long enough.

* * *

Casey didn't have his jacket with him as he helped Susan set out the hot dogs, buns and all the trimmings on the tables at Shaughnessy Park that afternoon — but he was still thinking about it. It was the last day of the Summer Fun Program for Shaughnessy. Casey set the basket with the plastic ketchup and mustard packets on the table and sat down to watch. Out on the playing field the kids were having a water balloon derby. Casey knew them by name now. He liked all of them — even old yellow shirt, the eternal skeptic. And, of course, he especially liked May. Whatever he did, the good tricks and the not-so-good, May had always believed.

"They're having a great time, aren't they?" said Susan.

"Water balloons were always my favourite part too," said Casey. "Susan?"

"What?"

"Could you give something to May for me?" Casey slipped off his pack and removed a brown paper bag. I'm not very good at giving presents. It's my old magic kit."

"Sure," said Susan. "I understand. But you're still going to stay for the party, aren't you? We'd all like you to. You were the hit of the session!"

"It was fun," said Casey, "but, no, I don't think I'll stay."

Susan sat on the bench beside him.

"I gather people aren't exactly banging down your door to see Casey Webber the Great."

"I'm still working on it," said Casey.

"Good," said Susan. "You know your act is a bit unconventional. It's even a little scary how you do things without any place for props or wires or anything. Sometimes, when I watch, I find my mind wants to kind of slip away and say 'that can't be happening, so it isn't.' It's a very strange feeling. But then I look at the children and they're entranced by it all and I know it is happening. I think, if you ever got a chance just to be up there, on a big stage, where people really expect magic . . . Casey?"

"What?" asked Casey.

"Never mind. Come on. Stay for the eats. It's almost time."

Casey shook his head. He took a couple of ketchup packages from one of the boxes as a souvenir for his collection. Then, with a wave, he jumped on his bike and rode away.

Chapter Eight

"We need him and we need him now!" said Max.

He and T.J. were standing on the doorstep when Morgan opened the door.

"If you mean Casey, he isn't here," said Morgan.

"He's got to be here. Only the world's greatest magician can save us!" said T.J.

"What's wrong?" asked Morgan.

"They're after us. The whole Lidden Street gang," said Max. "You know what a great ride it is coming down Lidden Hill? Well, all the kids up there decided it's their hill and nobody else could ride it."

"But Max wouldn't stand for it," cut in T.J. "Not Max. He got his bike out and went around the long way and pushed, sly as a fox, up through the trees. It was like one of those shows where the good guy sneaks up from behind."

"Except I had my bike," said Max.

"Except he had his bike," said T.J. "And when he got to the top of the hill he didn't just come down, you see. He waited and waited. And waited until every single Lidden Hill kid was there swarming all over the place and acting tough and then he yelled..."

"Geronimo!" Max demonstrated. "And I came flying out of the bushes and like an eagle down the hill..."

"Just like an eagle..." continued T.J., "an eagle at 180 kilometers an hour down the hill and around the corner. It was wonderful. I was with him."

"On your bike?" asked Morgan.

"No, on his bike," said T.J. "On the handlebars."

"At 180 kilometers an hour down Lidden Hill?"

"I had my eyes closed all the way," said T.J.

"You're crazy," said Morgan. "You're both crazy."

"No, we're dead," said Max. "Every kid from Lidden Street is looking for us. We need Casey."

"Oh, right. You really need Casey. He's a real fighter."

"We need him to turn them into stone, or teach us to fly, or blow all their bike tires. We don't care what he does, so long as he does it. Where is he?"

"Shaughnessy Park," said Morgan.

"Right," said Max.

He and T.J. took off on their bikes. Morgan's mom was just coming up the walk.

"Was that a herd of buffalo or just Max and T.J.?" she asked.

"Buffalo," said Morgan. "Casey has the strangest friends."

She took a bag of groceries from her mom and together they went into the house and set the groceries on the kitchen counter.

"Speaking of friends, I saw one of your friends over town," said Morgan's mom. "She said her name was Emily. Do you know what she was doing?"

"Oh no," said Morgan, her heart sinking. "You didn't turn her in for shoplifting!"

"She wasn't shoplifting," said Morgan's mom. "She was buying all sorts of crazy stuff. She was buying it, so she could —"

"Emily?" asked Morgan. "She was just pretending to lift the stuff?"

"Seems you're not the only one who doesn't want to lead a life of crime," said her mom. She picked up the letters on the counter and began to shuffle through them. When she got to the yellow and purple envelope she stopped. Her mouth drew into a tight line of concern.

"Not another one," she said. "Did they phone this one to us?"

Morgan shook her head. Mrs. Webber read the telegram.

"INTERFERENCE OVER AT LAST. ON MY WAY SOONEST.
S.V."

*　*　*

Casey was smiling as he pedalled home from Shaughnessy Park. He had just thought of the perfect magic act for the Tom Gregory Show. The way he saw it, since both "Entertainers at Large" and "Kids in the Spotlight" had turned him down, it was now almost certain that he would get a chance to be on the Tom Gregory Show. It had to happen, that was all there was to it. And he was going to be ready. He was going to be very much ready indeed.

"Casey. Caseeeeeeee!"

Max and T.J. were bombing towards him on their bikes. They slammed on the brakes and spun to a stop.

"Boy, are we glad to see you! You've got to help us," said T.J.

"The whole Lidden Street gang is after us," said Max, "Craig and Luke and all those guys. We've given them the slip twice this morning but I think one of them saw us just a few blocks back."

"They're going to kill us," said T.J.

"Why would they want to kill you?" asked Casey.

"No time to explain. Look!"

Far down the end of the street three riders were pedalling hard in their direction. Even as Max spoke a fourth joined them.

"The bad guys chasing the good guys," said T.J.

"Quick, Casey. Magic them," said Max.

"What?" asked Casey.

"Magic them. You know. Do an illusion. Make their bikes float or make us disappear or start a fire or something. Just like on T.V. You can do it. We've seen you. Quick!"

"But...but...but..."

The bike
riders were barely a block away
and a fifth had come in from a side street to
join them.

"Yikes!" said Casey. "Get going.
Somewhere. Anywhere. I'll think of something."

Max and T.J. jumped on their bikes
and went racing down the street. Casey stood a moment waiting
for inspiration
to hit
him.

Nothing hit, so he jumped on his bike and raced after Max and T.J.

Down 48th Street they sped, through the back of the grocery and west across the boulevard. Max, T.J. and Casey had the advantage of knowing the neighbourhood, but there were more of the other kids and they were bigger. Every time Max, T.J. and Casey seemed to have gained some breathing room from one batch of their pursuers, they'd turn to find the other half closing in from another side.

Casey didn't know what he was going to do. Max and T.J. were counting on him. He didn't even have the jacket, but he had to do something. If only there were time to think! Casey heard the distant whine of sirens. He put on a burst of speed and drew up alongside Max.

"Follow me," he called and turned down the road that led to Hospital Bridge.

The ambulance had just crossed the bridge and was screaming up the hill when Craig Snope, leader of the Lidden Street gang, came over the last rise before the river. Craig liked ambulances. He slowed down and watched a moment before looking for the kids he was chasing. Even after the ambulance had gone, he didn't spot them right away. He was looking for a moving quarry — three kids pedalling like mad. Instead, what he spotted was a splash of yellow that was the fluorescent frame of T.J.'s bike on the rocks above the river.

Several other boys joined Craig at his lookout. Down the hill they rode. When they got a little closer they could see that something was wrong. The bike wasn't in one piece. It was all mixed up with Max's and Casey's bikes. Pieces were strewn all over and everywhere, and generally smashed to smithereens on the rocks.

Max and T.J. were nowhere around, but their friend was there. He was sitting limply on a rock looking at the bikes and shaking his head. His hair was rumpled, his shirt was ripped, there was a big smudge of dirt across his face. He was holding Max's grease-smeared sneaker in one hand and T.J.'s hat in the other.

Craig and his friends rode up and surveyed the wreckage of tangled bikes and pieces of bikes, scattered scraps of clothing.

"What happened?" asked Craig.

Casey blinked at him with a blank expression.

"Wipe-out," he said. "It had to happen sooner or later, you know. Those two were maniacs on their bikes."

"Is that blood?" asked one of the kids, pointing to a long red smear on one of the rocks.

Casey turned slowly to look at it.

"I don't know. I guess so. Poor T.J." he said.

"Is he ... alive?" asked Craig.

"Boy oh boy. They must have really creamed themselves," said Craig. "They should have just let us catch them. We wouldn't have hurt them or anything. All we wanted to do was scare them."

"Why?" asked Casey.

"To keep them off Lidden Hill," said Craig. "The police are going to ban bikes from the hill entirely if kids like Max and T.J. don't stop racing down."

"Well," said Casey, shaking his head, "I don't think they'll even be thinking about Lidden Hill for a long, long time."

"Look," said Craig, "do you want some help or something to get the bikes home?"

"No, that's okay. The ambulance people said they'd phone my dad. He should be here soon," said Casey.

"Are you sure?" asked Craig. "We could just keep you company."

Casey shook his head.

"Take care of yourself," said Craig.

He and his friends set off back the way they'd come. Casey sat and watched them until they were out of sight. He stood up and began to put the bikes back together. Actually, it was only T.J.'s bike that had to go back together. T.J.'s bike was the only one with quick releases on the wheels and seat, but mixed in with the other two bikes it made it look like all of them were broken. Max and T.J. hopped sock-footed out of their hiding place beneath the bridge.

"Why didn't they just tell us about the police on Lidden Hill?" asked T.J. "We would have stopped racing."

"I don't know," said Casey.

Max picked up his shoes and cap and the ripped patch from his jeans.

"T.J. and I were talking under the

bridge," said Max. "We're sorry about the magic bit. I guess we got carried away. It wasn't fair asking you to magic them. I mean, this isn't T.V., is it? On T.V. there's a cast of thousands figuring out how the tricks are going to work."

"And they stop the cameras and have all sorts of special effects and bomb-proof suits and air bags and spend a million dollars. It's just that your magic tricks are so neat, they almost seem as if... they're real," said T.J., "but, of course, they're just tricks. Anybody knows that."

Casey put his lips tightly together. He would love to show them the jacket. He would really love to take them home and show them. And why not? Weren't they his best friends?

"The way you saved our skins was twice as neat anyway," said Max. "Did you hear him, T.J.? Here, I'll fix my bike. Hand me the wheel."

Casey handed him the wheel. He sat on the rock and watched his friends put themselves and their bikes back together. The feeling that he wanted to show them the jacket passed. Max and T.J. were the greatest friends a kid could have, but they belonged in the real world. Casey was part of the real world too. That was the feeling Morgan had been trying to explain — the believing and not believing. No, the jacket wasn't for blabbing about.

"Let's head home," said Casey.

Chapter Nine

"Casey? I've been trying every Webber in the phone book and I'd almost run out of them," said the voice on the phone. "It's Susan, Susan from Shaughnessy Park."

"Is something wrong?" asked Casey.

"Nothing's wrong," said Susan. "Have you ever heard of the city's Summer Festival?"

"I think so," said Casey. "It's kind of a fair with folk singers and bands and dancers."

"Right. The city sponsors it every summer on the outdoor stage at Central Park," said Susan. "The gate money goes to recreational programs and the acts perform for free, but that doesn't mean it's small time. These are some of the best acts in this area. A large crowd comes every year. You're in it."

"I'm what?" asked Casey.

"You're in it. Sunday. This Sunday.

There's always a few cancellations at the last minute and you're one of the fillers."

"I don't understand..." said Casey.

"We nominated you — the kids and I. We carried 28 signs and an eight foot banner reading 'Casey Webber, World's Greatest Magician' into the city recreation department offices," said Susan.

"And they said okay?" asked Casey.

"How could they resist 30 exuberant kids and their determined camp counsellor?" said Susan. "You have to report backstage on Sunday at 10:00 a.m. They'll give you your time slot then. And Casey?"

"Yes?"

"You're welcome," said Susan.

The line went dead. Casey stood holding the receiver. Something inside him did a double flip.

"Yahoo!" he shouted. "Yahoo! Yippee!"

He raced into the living room. His mom and dad were sitting side by side on the sofa.

"Yahoo!" he said, and without explanation raced down to Morgan's room.

"The Summer Festival?" asked Morgan when Casey had told her the news.

"Yes, yes," said Casey. "It's perfect. It's exactly what I've been waiting for. It's my big chance!"

"Casey, I don't think..." began Morgan.

"I've got it all planned. I'll need your help. The lady at 'Entertainers at Large' was right. What I had was a bunch of tricks kind of mish-mashed together and that isn't what the act is really about. What the act is about is the jacket. And what the jacket is about is..."

"Casey, will you listen to me!" interrupted Morgan. "You can't do the show. Any show."

"Why not?" asked Casey.

"Because the jacket isn't yours!" said Morgan. She reached across the desk for the old photo album she'd found among the jigsaw puzzles. She opened it at the spot where she'd tucked a kleenex in. "It's his."

Casey leaned forward and looked at the photo. It was taken in their back yard when the trees were smaller and Morgan herself was still small enough to be riding her trike on the cement pad in the background. Several people were gathered talking. There was one man in particular — a tallish, solidly built man who might have been fat if he hadn't been holding himself so straight. He was wearing grey flannel pants, a shirt and vest and a beret, but it was the face Casey noticed.

"It's him!" said Casey.

"Who?" asked Morgan.

"From the picture you dropped in my room," said Casey.

"What picture?" asked Morgan.

"The day you first tried on the jacket and didn't know you were invisible, you dropped something. It was a metal case with a picture in it."

"No I didn't," said Morgan.

"But it had to come from you. I'd checked the pockets on the jacket that morning. They were empty," said Casey.

"Do you still have it?" asked Morgan.

Casey went to his own room and returned with the small metal case.

"See," he said, laying it down beside the photo album. "It's him."

"Casey," said Morgan, "Casey, this doesn't make sense. I don't know if this is a photograph or some kind of very small, faded painting but I do know one thing. It's old.

Really old. I mean this guy would have to be 100 . . . or 200 . . . now, or . . . something . . ."

"Well, okay. It's not him. But it sure looks like him. A lot."

"A lot," said Morgan. "Did you see what he's holding?"

Casey bent forward to look more closely at the picture in the photo album. Over his arm the man was holding a jacket. It was a dark jacket with a high collar and buttons down the front, just like Casey's.

Casey frowned. "Who is it?" he asked.

"I'm not sure. Mom and Dad say the picture was taken at a lawn party they had with some of the neighbours and they think he was someone's guest," said Morgan. "Take this magnifying glass and look at the crest on the jacket."

Casey saw that exactly where the dark spot was on his own jacket, there was indeed a crest on the jacket in the photograph. The letters were very small but Casey thought he could just make them out.

"S.V.," said Casey. He could almost feel his heart sinking. "The telegrams."

"'LEAVE WELL ENOUGH ALONE. STOP ACTION. ARRIVING SOONEST.' Casey, he's been trying to tell us all along," said Morgan.

Casey looked at the picture again and then he looked at Morgan.

"It doesn't matter," he said.

"Casey..." began Morgan.

"It doesn't matter. Don't you see?" said Casey. "Maybe we do know whose jacket it is, and maybe he's expecting to get it back, but he isn't here yet. The jacket is still in my dresser drawer. It's still mine to use."

"Casey..." Morgan tried again.

"This is my big chance, Morgan," said Casey. "It may be my only chance. I'm not robbing a bank or scaring people or trading secrets with the enemy. I'm not doing anything spectacularly bad. I'm not doing anything spectacularly good either. It's a magic act — that's all — but... maybe, just maybe, it's worth something all on its own."

The room was quiet, and Casey added hopefully, "I might not trip over the sleigh this time!"

Morgan looked at her brother. Things had been a lot simpler when she'd been the world's most sarcastic sister and he'd just been her dippy little brother. Really, she thought, people should just go from being babies to being adults and skip this growing up stuff.

"Will you help me, Morgan?" asked Casey. "Please."

* * *

The performances had already started on Sunday morning when Casey and Morgan arrived at Central Park. The area was decorated with flags and banners. Booths selling food and handicrafts were strung gaily in a line beneath the trees at one end of the open area. At the other end was the outdoor stage with its high roof, solid timbers and larger than life backdrop on which were painted, like a mirror image, the tall trees of the park itself.

Between the stage and the booths were people — lots of people. All across the grass in front of the stage, many, many rows deep, they lay and sat and picnicked and listened to the music. Behind this sweeping crowd more people wandered in and out among the booths — visiting, eating, looking. And even as Casey surveyed the scene, more people were arriving to enjoy it.

Casey and Morgan made their way to the blue and white tent behind the outdoor stage. The manager gave them an afternoon time slot for their performance. They left their bags of props beside the tent. Morgan went off to buy something to drink. Casey put on the jacket.

Casey had never been invisible in the midst of a crowd of people before. He had the oddest feeling of freedom, the sensation of being part of something larger than himself without being there at all.

On the stage, two people were singing Irish ballads. Casey wanted to be certain the jacket worked on stage as well as off. He went around to the rear and climbed up behind the electrical equipment and around the backstage crew. He took a deep breath and poked his head around the backdrop. He put one arm out. He put one leg out. He put his whole body out, so he was standing in what should have been full view just at the side of the stage.

Little by little Casey nudged further and further on stage. Finally he stood front and centre between the two folk singers. The energy of their voices and instruments rushed like wind around him and through him. He looked out across the crowd, carefully searching for a sign that someone, anyone, knew he was there. When he was satisfied that not one single person saw even a shadow of Casey Webber, he turned and left the stage.

Well, he almost left the stage. Just at the

edge he paused and looked out one last time. It was in those few small moments that he recognized someone in the audience. No, it was not just one person. It was two people, still standing some distance apart, but they had at that moment spotted each other as well.

Morgan was waiting with a concerned expression on her face when Casey returned to the tent.

"A little girl was just here," she said, not waiting for Casey to explain where he'd been. "She asked if I knew Casey the Magician and I said yes, and she asked me to give you this. She was pretty upset about something."

Casey looked in the bag and saw his old magic kit. May!

"Do you know who it was?" asked Morgan. "She was awfully upset."

"May Tanagami from Shaughnessy Park — I told you about her, remember? When was she here?" he asked.

"Just a few minutes ago," said Morgan. "Her mother asked her if she was sure she didn't want to stay and watch the show, but she just took off."

"Which way?" asked Casey.

"Towards the parking lot," said Morgan.

Quickly Casey set off around the stage,

through the edge of the crowd. He could see May and her mom walking side by side towards the cars.

"May! May!"

She turned. The look on her face surprised Casey. Instead of its usual warm welcome her face held a closed and troubled expression. Casey held out the bag.

"I didn't mean for you to give this back, you know. You can keep it. It's yours," said Casey.

"I don't want it," said May. "It's... it's not real."

"Sure it is," said Casey. "There's lots of neat things in it!"

May shook her head.

"It doesn't do real magic," said May.

May's mother dropped to one knee beside her.

"Oh May," she said. "Is that what this is all about?"

She turned to Casey apologetically.

"I'm sorry, young man," she said. "May just doesn't understand that magic is tricks; very well done tricks."

"Not Casey's magic," said May.

She turned to look up at him. "You do do real magic. It is real, isn't it?"

Casey stood very quietly. He had a sick feeling in the pit of his stomach.

"Come May," said her mother.

May looked at Casey for one last long, hopeful minute, then she turned away.

"I'm sorry," said her mother. "She'll get over it. I'll explain it to her. I'm sorry to make you feel bad."

But Casey was not thinking about how he felt, he was thinking about how May was feeling. Of all the people he'd shown his tricks to, she alone had really believed.

"Wait," said Casey. "Wait."

He looked around him and pulled May and her mother closer to one of the big trees.

"May, listen to me. I can do one thing that is magic — one thing only. I can't do anything else. I can't make trees grow or sick people get well or cars fly. I'm not really magic myself. I don't know anyone who is and I don't know how long it's going to last. I just happened to find something that was magic. Do you understand?"

May nodded.

"Okay," said Casey. "Watch this."

There on the grass in front of May and her mother, Casey put on his jacket. He didn't need to ask if it worked. He could tell by the look on both their faces — the delight in May's eyes and the complete amazement in her mother's.

"It's not a trick and it's not a science, at least not that I know of," said Casey's voice from mid air. "It's just plain magic. Care to shake hands with Mr. Invisible, May?"

May put out her hand first and Casey soundly shook it.

"Mrs. Tanagami?" asked Casey.

May looked at her mom and she, too, hesitatingly put out her hand to be shaken. At that moment something bumped Casey from behind and sent him sprawling to the grass.

"Was that Casey?" asked Morgan, out of breath.

"Crumb, Morgan, you almost killed me," said Casey, coming into view.

"There's been a change. They want us on stage. Now!"

Casey looked at May. She smiled her warmest smile. Casey held out the magic trick box.

"Keep it just for fun," he said.

Together he and Morgan turned and raced away. May and her mother watched them until they were over the crest of the small hill, then they followed.

Chapter Ten

"*L*adies and Gentlemen, please give a warm welcome to Casey and Morgan Webber and an act they call — MR. INVISIBLE!"

It felt like being in a dream, thought Casey, as he stood looking out over the crowd, an amazing dream. A great sea of faces spread before him. Thousands of hands clapped their welcome. Bodies of all shapes and sizes shifted into positions of comfort. All eyes settled upon the very spot where he and Morgan stood.

"Psst. Casey."

Casey turned. Morgan was holding out a bright red baseball cap. Casey took the cap and put it on his head and the dream that wasn't a dream began to move.

They had set up their magic chamber on the left side of the stage. It was a blanketed tepee elevated on a low table. Slowly, savouring every moment, Casey crossed the stage to the table. With a grand salute to Morgan and the crowd before him, he entered the magic chamber.

There was a moment of quiet in the audience, a small drawing together of expectancy. It was an important moment. The crowd could be won or lost in those few short seconds. At just the right instant the hat emerged from the other side of the tepee.

It didn't come flying out, it just came out. It was looking down at first, then it turned and seemed to look at the audience. Once again it looked down and in a swift, sure movement it dropped a foot in space and there was a thump as if, well, as if someone had jumped from the table to the stage. For another deliciously long moment the hat hung suspended in space. Then it began to float.

Casey didn't see the small smiles that spread through the audience as the hat floated with a gentle, bouncing gait across the stage, but with some strange sense he could feel the warmth that was being directed at the stage. The hat floated left. It floated right. It stopped beside Morgan.

Morgan reached into her bag and took out two running boots. She knelt on the stage beneath the hat, wiggled them back and forth each in turn, and tied their laces. She stood up again and stepped back. For a moment that's all there was. Hat. Runners.

Then one of the runners lifted by itself. Up, down, up, down. The runners began to walk with the hat bouncing along above. A wave of delighted amusement swept across the audience. The runners gained confidence. They began to stride and jump and finally race full speed around the stage. They screeched to a halt at Morgan's side, jumped up and clicked their heels. laughter and applause swept up from the audience.

"Ham," said Morgan.

Morgan reached into the bag and took out a pair of gloves. She held the left one out below the hat and above the runners. It wiggled a moment and was still. She let go. The glove remained suspended quietly in mid-air.

Count of one.

Count of two.

The glove began to move: up, down, sideways, turn, drop, fan, roll, and swirl. There was an elegance in the movements, the wonderful fluid elegance of the human body that is as evident in the simplest of movements as in the most complex. In the audience no one turned to speak to each other because each was suddenly sure that they were not watching puppets or machines or tricks of lights and motion but something that was really there alive before them, a glimpse of something that could only be believed in when you were completely, totally certain that it did not exist at all.

Morgan held out the other glove. The same thing happened. Both hands were going up and down, back and forth. One toe began to tap. The hands began to clap.

Clap. Clap, clap. Clap.
Tap. Tap, tap. Tap.
The hat and
gloves and
runners
began

to dance around the stage in time to the beat. Morgan took up the rhythm and, without even being aware of it, the audience began to clap too.

Clap. Clap,clap. Clap.

Mr. Invisible was alive and well and dancing across the stage.

For more than fifteen minutes, long past the time allotted to him, Mr. Invisible delighted the large crowd of people gathered in the park that afternoon. He put on a vest and pair of shorts. He skipped, jumped and tossed tennis balls back and forth with Morgan. He hula-hooped and walked on his hands and juggled. When at last Morgan removed his

gloves and boots and the hat floated back into the magic chamber, it was to a great roar of applause. So great was the applause that Morgan had to hold up her hands for the act was not yet over.

The clapping stopped. Casey was in the magic chamber. Morgan walked slowly to the microphone.

"To end our show we wanted you to know that the amazing Mr. Invisible is a real person in every way so we thought we'd have him reappear in the audience this time — right...about...there!"

Morgan pointed to the pre-arranged place. All heads turned. Count of one. Count of two. But no Casey stood up.

"Casey?" asked Morgan into the mike. "Casey?"

A cold little chill swept down Morgan's back.

"Casey?" she called out over the audience. There was real fear in her stomach now. Hadn't she known something would happen? Hadn't it been her job to stop him before it was too late?

A murmur from the people before her drew her attention back to the audience. She could feel their uncertainty. The moment had been stretched as long as it could. Soon the magic would break away. The show would end on a flat and sour note.

It was too good a show to end that way. Casey had tried too hard and performed well. Morgan pushed her own fears aside. She raised her arms in a shrug that was sure and swift and larger than life.

"Well, ladies and gentlemen," she said. "He's out there somewhere. If you find him, send him home in time for supper."

As if nothing could be more normal than an invisible brother who was always late for supper, Morgan grabbed the gunny sack, and the props and left the stage. She had done the best she could. The applause that followed her was warm and real. When she went back to get the invisible chamber, lifting the flap to expose it to the audience and shaking her head to find it empty before carting it away, she knew the act had ended as it should have ended — without even the smallest of tricks.

There was only one thing wrong.

Casey was really missing.

Chapter Eleven

"*H*ey Morgan!"

Max and T.J. were running across the grass behind the stage. Morgan had never been so glad to see Max and T.J. as she was at this moment.

"It was great," called Max. "Really great. Where's Mr. Invisible?"

"I don't know," said Morgan. "Something's gone..."

"What an act!" said T.J., coming up close on Max's heels. "I almost couldn't believe it. My friend Casey Webber, the amazing, the astounding, the fantastic Mr. Invisible."

"It was like magic out there in the crowd," said Max. "What do you mean you don't know where he is?"

"I'm trying to tell you. He's disappeared and —"

"And how!" interrupted T.J. "Give me

a hint — the tiniest hint. It's done with holograms, isn't it?"

"Will you listen to me — " pleaded Morgan.

"Real magicians don't reveal their secrets to anyone," said Max. "Right, Morgan?"

"There is no secret," said Morgan. "There's just the jacket and Casey's got it on and I don't know where he is and you guys have got to help me find him, because Casey could be in real trouble."

"How could he be in trouble?" asked T.J. "They loved him out there. When he danced across the stage, and juggled and played the harmonica..."

"And the ending — the ending was great," said Max. "There are little kids out there actually wandering around looking for Mr. Invisible."

"That's what I mean," said Morgan. "He's really gone!"

"Great idea," said T.J. "Are you going to have the announcer send out lost and found messages?"

Morgan threw her hands up in exasperation.

"Listen to me! Casey is invisible. Really invisible. And he's missing. And..."

"And his disappearance, his final disappearance of the afternoon, was not part of the act."

It was a stern voice. Morgan, Max and T.J. turned around to find a man standing beside them. He was a tall, solidly built man who might have been fat if not for the way he held himself so straight. He wore a beret, a sweater and grey flannel pants, and a neatly trimmed beard.

Morgan knew him. She knew him not just from the picture in the old photo album but, now that he stood before her, she knew him from her own memory as well. Half-remembered images came rushing to her. She did not have time to sort them into good and bad.

"What have you done with Casey?" she demanded.

The man's brows lowered and his eyes were like small, black rocks.

"I'd have rather thought the question was what has Casey done with MY jacket," he said darkly.

"The jacket with the hologram equipment?" asked T.J.

The man turned a menacing look upon T.J., and Morgan stepped quickly between them. He glared down at her.

"Do you know what you and your brother have done, young lady?" he de-

manded. "You have ridiculed an article of the ancient magic. You have used it for games — childish games, tricks, the amusement of the common rabble. A jacket that was once worn by a sultan's son! A jacket that was once the key to an empress' power! A jacket that saved a king from death and an entire kingdom from slipping into slavery. A jacket that..."

" ...sat in someone's closet for the last 300 years doing sweet tweet," finished a voice at their elbow and Mrs. Armstrong stepped into the circle. She was wearing her special lemonade hat and carried her oversize purse. She looked across at the large man. "Really, Syl, I won't have you browbeating the children," she said. "Morgan, do you remember Mr. Voss?"

"Very well, I'll browbeat you instead,"

said Sylvester Voss, ignoring the introduction and turning on Mrs. Armstrong. "You're the one that put me up to this. 'Two of the nicest children imaginable,' you told me. 'I'll be here to watch over them and how could it hurt' you said. 'The jacket will be like a small spark, around which their imagination might leap like a splendid flame'. Very poetic. And when they got old enough to take the flame and run with it, did you even try to stop them?"

Sylvester Voss pointed a short, stout finger.

"You've been right in there all along, cheering them on!" he said.

"I did not interfere," said Mrs. Armstrong.

"You didn't stop them!" continued Sylvester Voss undaunted. "You don't fool me, Clarissa Armstrong. There is no place in the modern world for magic and I should never have fallen for that fiddle-faddle talk of yours about creative imagination. That jacket and I have been together for a long time and I knew the instant these children had begun to use it for their own small-minded ends. I had a terrible time getting here, and only sheer luck let me find out about this performance, but here I am now and..."

"And what?" interrupted Mrs. Armstrong. "All you can do is rant and pout and throw your arms around. If you'd think, really think, you'd see that the jacket has been used very nicely..."

"Very nicely!" roared Sylvester Voss. "Very NICELY! That jacket was once worn by the greatest king that — "

"You cannot live in the past, Syl. There are things to be done here and now by regular people and — "

"Stop," cried Morgan. "Stop. Please stop."

Both parties looked down at the young girl who stood defiantly between them.

"Where IS Casey?"

Mrs. Armstrong glanced at Max, T.J., Sylvester Voss and then back to Morgan. "You mean... you really don't know?" she asked.

"No," said Morgan.

"Oh dear," said Mrs. Armstrong, drawing suddenly very quiet. Sylvester Voss sniffed soundly and drew himself up.

"You see," he said. "You see what happens when the ordinary rabble get it?"

"Where is Casey?" demanded Morgan. "Have you done something to him? Has he had an accident? He could be lying half dead somewhere and no one could even see to help him."

"No, no." Mrs. Armstrong put a reassuring hand on Morgan's arm. "The jacket can take care of itself. He might get knocked around a bit now and again but, no, if he's not here, it's because he doesn't want to be here."

"He's run away with it!" said Max.

Morgan turned to Max, and Max raised his hands.

"Don't listen to me. I don't even know what you're talking about. Sometimes I just say things."

Morgan looked at Sylvester Voss and Mrs. Armstrong. It was easy enough to see that was exactly what they thought had happened and that they took such an action very seriously.

"He must not be pursued," the large man said to Mrs. Armstrong. "You know that. The jacket must be freely given, freely returned. Even at this moment, as he runs with it, the magic will be changing into something small and mean. The jacket will become something to be owned, something just the opposite of all it is meant to be."

"But Casey wouldn't just run off with it!" said Morgan. "He understood that it was something special. No matter how much he wanted the jacket for his own, he wouldn't just run off with it."

"There is no other possible explanation," announced Mr. Voss. "There are dangers you do not even know about. It cannot be allowed."

He raised his arm, his fist a tight ball of energy.

"Stop!" said Morgan.

"Sylvester!" said Mrs. Armstrong sternly.

"The boy will not be hurt," said Sylvester Voss, "but the jacket . . . it is one of the great jokes on mankind that neither you nor I can make a flower grow without seed and soil and sun, but we can uproot it with a mere twist of the wrist. And I must do it now, before it is a moment too late."

The fist at the end of the arm opened. The five fingers spread wide, wide. The moment hung suspended — count of one, count of two . . .

"Here he comes!" shouted T.J. "Here comes Casey!"

Sylvester Voss and Morgan spun around.

"Where?" cried Morgan. "Where?"

T.J. pointed past the blue and white tent. For a moment they saw nothing, and then their minds picked out what was there not to be seen. Two hot dogs and two full sized raspberry slushes were bounding along at a jolly clip about a metre above the grass. They zoomed and careened among the trees, zipped unnoticed behind a passing group of people and twirled to a stand-still before Max, T.J., Morgan, Mrs. Armstrong and Sylvester Voss.

"I would have been here sooner but I had to go back and get the relish," said Casey's voice from mid-air. "Hold these, could you?"

Morgan reached out her hands and took the hot dogs and slushes. A moment later Casey himself slid into view.

His face was flushed from running and his voice seemed almost breezy. Only Morgan, who knew him so well, was aware of the emotion in his eyes.

"I don't suppose I could keep it even for a little longer?" asked Casey. "A day? A week? A year or two?"

"No," said Sylvester Voss.

"Well," said Casey. "Well."

He drew a deep breath and held out the jacket. Although he was a good deal smaller than the man in every way, for just a moment they seemed to look levelly across at each other.

"It is a very fine jacket and it has been a privilege to use it," said Casey.

And the invisible jacket changed hands.

Chapter Twelve

Casey Webber sat on the front steps of his house with a long white envelope unopened in his hands. The envelope bore the distinctive logo of the Tom Gregory Show. Casey was trying to decide whether the envelope held an invitation or a rejection, just how disappointed he should be in either case, and whether or not to open it at all.

The jacket was gone. He and Morgan had watched from their yard only that morning as Sylvester Voss strode down the walk from Mrs. Armstrong's house, climbed into a taxi and departed. There had been not a glance in their direction, not a word of explanation. All that was left now was the letter.

The door behind Casey opened and

Mrs. Armstrong stepped out onto the landing.

"I just wanted to be certain everything was cleared up," she said. "I know that Syl's apologies can be rather... abrupt."

Casey's mother spoke from the doorway.

"Well, you're right. His explanation came across more like a royal decree than an apology. I still don't understand what it was all about, but at least there won't be any more telegrams."

They talked for a moment longer. Then the door closed and Mrs. Armstrong came down the steps carefully, one at a time. Casey put the envelope into his pocket and walked with her down the front drive.

"Is he really gone?" asked Casey.

"Oh yes, he's gone," said Mrs. Armstrong.

"Was he really 300 years old?" asked Casey.

"It depends on where and how you count the years," said Mrs. Armstrong. "If you count them our way, then he is very much older than 300, but if you count them his way then he couldn't be much more than 62, 63 at the most. He's been in his late 50's and early 60's for most of my life, but of course, I'm older than he is now. Which reminds me, you didn't happen to keep..."

Casey took the small metal picture case from his pocket.

"You put it in the pocket, didn't you?" he said, handing it to her.

"It did seem to me that if you were going to champion the magic you should have some idea who was at the other end. It wouldn't have been wise for me to do more, but I did what I could," said Mrs. Armstrong. "Thank you for keeping it, Casey. It's been in my family a long time."

She set the case gently in the bottom of her purse.

"Do you think he will ever come back?" asked Casey.

"He has been the mysterious, long lost relative in our family for ever so many years and he and I are friends in our own way. Yes, I expect he'll be back for a visit," said Mrs. Armstrong. "But if you are thinking what I think you are thinking, the answer is no. We will not see the jacket again. We poked a few holes in his arguments but, all in all, old people like Syl and me are very slow to change."

She stopped and looked at Casey. A smile played at the corners of her mouth.

"Besides, when something is done properly the first time," she said, "it doesn't need doing again."

Casey tried not to show his disappointment. There were a million questions he wanted to ask, but he knew there were going to be no answers.

"By the way, Syl was gracious enough to give me a few newspaper clippings that might interest you. I left them inside with your sister," said Mrs. Armstrong. "Just now, however, I think I'll wander down the block and see if anyone has set up a lemonade stand. I could use a glass of lemonade on a hot day like this."

So saying, Mrs. Armstrong headed off down the street. Casey stood and watched her go. He took the envelope with the Tom Gregory logo out of his back pocket, walked to the garbage bin by the garage and dropped it in.

The front door banged open and Morgan came down the steps with a handful of newspaper clippings.

"Casey, have you seen these?" she asked.

"I don't want to see them," said Casey.

"Yes, you do," said Morgan.

"No, I don't," said Casey. He sat on the

steps again. "I don't want to remember how it might have been or how some other people thought it was. I'm just going to remember the jacket my way."

"But Casey..." said Morgan.

Casey raised his hand.

"It's all right. You don't have to try and make me feel better." He looked out across the street, but it wasn't houses he was seeing. He was seeing a crowd of people with their eyes riveted on his every move. "It was just grand all in itself, Morgan. It was the chance of a lifetime — being up there on stage. You know I thought the best part would be being famous and everyone knowing me and thinking I was great but the best part was ..."

" ... showing people something quite magical," finished Morgan. There was a moment of silence and then Morgan said quietly, "You really were going to run off with the jacket, weren't you?"

"But I didn't," said Casey. "I can't explain why. There was just something about the jacket — it wasn't ours to run off with. What the heck. Let me see those newspaper clippings. I might as well live it all over again in newsprint since I'm not going to live it any other way."

"But that's what I've been trying to tell you," said Morgan. "These aren't clippings about the act. Here — read them."

She thrust the clippings into Casey's hands. As he leafed through them one name repeated itself over and over:

At today's official cere-mony May Tanagami, 83, win-ner of the Nobel Prize for Physics...

May Tanagami, prize winning physicist for her work dedicated to the preservation of a precious planet...

The award was accepted by 83 year old physicist, May Tanagami...

"I don't understand," said Casey.

"May Tanagami," said Morgan. "The little girl from Shaughnessy Park."

"May's not 83 years old! She's six or maybe seven at the most," said Casey.

"She's not always going to be six. There are no dates on these clippings," said Morgan.

"But..."

"Casey, look!"

Casey read where Morgan pointed.

In her acceptance speech, Ms. Tanagami thanked a long list of people for their assistance over the years. Most especially she thanked a boy named Casey who, long ago, had the kindness to show her that in a world of so much disillusionment, all things are still possible.

Casey looked at Morgan and Morgan looked at Casey. For one long, rich moment a larger world and a line of time not usually contemplated touched them both. And Casey the Great understood that he was indeed part of something larger and greater. Even without magic, he had always belonged. And always would belong.

"I like that," said Casey. "That 'all things are still possible' bit."

"It kind of catches the imagination, doesn't it?" said Morgan.

"Caseeeeeeeee!"

Casey and Morgan looked up the street. A tall, wheeled, four armed monster was flying fast towards them. Max was riding on T.J.'s shoulders and T.J. was riding on the yellow bike.

"Come down to the school yard. We're

going to spin wheelies!" called Max as they whizzed by.

"Either that or they're going to kill themselves," said Morgan. "You have the strangest friends."

But wheelies at the school yard sounded just right to Casey. He tucked the newspaper clippings into his pocket and jumped up.

"Want to come, Morgan?"

"I would hate to," said Morgan. "Besides, Emily and I are going to see a show. But Casey..."

"Yup?"

He'd taken his bike from the side of the house and was swinging aboard. Morgan raised her voice to be sure she was heard.

"If you happen to run into anything unusual down at the school yard — a secret passage, a magic carpet, a hat that —"

He was already half-way down the street but his words came ringing clearly back to her.

"You'll be the first to know!" he called.

And Casey and Morgan Webber went each their separate way.